MR.

NONSENSE

by Roger Hargreaves

Mr Nonsense had no sense at all.

Not a scrap.

I mean, he lived in a tree.

A tree!

Can you imagine?

"Why do you live in a tree?" Mr Happy asked him one day.

"Because," replied Mr Nonsense, "I tried living on the ground, but that was too high up, so I moved to a tree to be nearer the ground."

"What nonsense," snorted Mr Happy.

"Thank you," replied Mr Nonsense.

And, do you know what Mr Nonsense liked to eat?

Porridge!

Nothing wrong with that you might say.

But, porridge on toast!

Really!

"Why do you like porridge on toast?" Mr Nosey asked him one day.

"Because," replied Mr Nonsense, "I tried porridge sandwiches and I didn't like them!"

And, do you know where Mr Nonsense sleeps every night?

In a rowing boat!

In his bedroom.

In his house.

Up a tree.

"Why do you sleep in a rowing boat?" Mr Strong asked him one day.

"Because," replied Mr Nonsense, "I tried sleeping in a motor boat but it was somewhat uncomfortable!"

Mr Nonsense lives, as you might very well expect, in a country called Nonsenseland.

Now, I know somebody else who lives in Nonsenseland.

Do you?

That's right.

Mr Silly!

Mr Silly and Mr Nonsense were close friends and saw a lot of each other.

Mr Nonsense was often round at Mr Silly's house playing jigsaw puzzles.

They used to throw the pieces at each other!

How silly!

And Mr Silly was often round at Mr Nonsense's house playing cards.

They used to tear them up to see who could get the most pieces out of one card!

What nonsense!

However, this story is about the time it snowed in Nonsenseland.

It didn't very often snow, but one winter it did.

Now, tell me, what colour is snow?

No, in Nonsenseland, when it snows, it doesn't snow white snow.

It snows yellow snow!

Don't ask me why.

But it does.

Yellow snow!

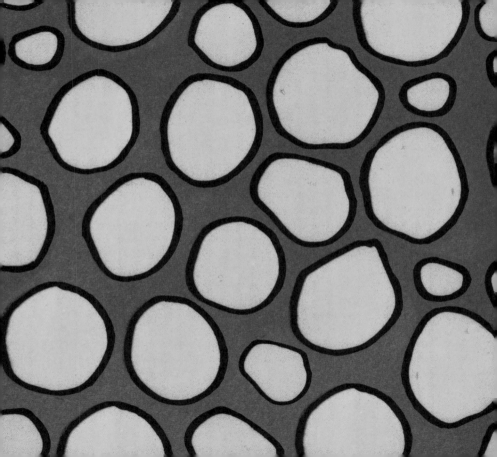

And, when Mr Silly woke up one morning, the whole of Nonsenseland was covered.

"I say," he said when he looked out of his bedroom window. "Snow!"

And he was so excited he rushed round to Mr Nonsense's house.

Mr Nonsense was asleep.

In his boat.

"Wake up!" cried Mr Silly. "Wake up, and come and look out of the window."

"What ever on earth is it?" grumbled Mr Nonsense, rubbing the sleep out of his eyes as he got up and went across to his bedroom window.

"I say," he said, looking out. "Custard!"

"That isn't custard, you silly banana," cried Mr Silly. "That's snow!"

He rushed downstairs.

"Come on," he called.

And that day, Mr Silly and Mr Nonsense had one of the very best days of their lives.

They had a snowball fight.

Mr Silly's snowballs were round.

Mr Nonsense made snowballs that somehow or other came out sort of square!

They built a snowman.

A very silly nonsensical sort of a snowman.

"Come on," said Mr Nonsense that afternoon. "Let's go tobogganing!"

"But we don't have a toboggan," said Mr Silly.

"Oh no, we don't," agreed Mr Nonsense.

Mr Silly thought.

"Oh yes, we do," he cried.

And Mr Silly ran back to Mr Nonsense's house, and came back with his bed.

"Wheeeee!" they shouted together as they slid faster and faster down the hill in their rowing boat toboggan.

It was a wonderful day.

And that evening, after having supper together (porridge pie), Mr Nonsense suggested that they played a game.

"What shall we play?" asked Mr Silly.

"Draughts," suggested Mr Nonsense.

"I've forgotten how to play draughts," said Mr Silly.

"Oh, it's easy," replied Mr Nonsense.

And went round and opened all the doors and windows!

"There we are," he said. "Draughts!"

What nonsense!

Fantastic offers for Mr. Men fans!

Collect all your Mr. Men or Little Miss books in these superb durable collectors' cases!
Only £5.99 inc. postage and packing, these wipe-clean, hard-wearing cases will give all your Mr. Men or Little Miss books a beautiful new home!

Keep track of your collection with this giant-sized double-sided Mr. Men and Little Miss Collectors' poster.
Collect 6 tokens and we will send you a brilliant giant-sized double-sided collectors' poster! Simply tape a £1 coin to cover postage and packaging in the space provided and fill out the form overleaf.

STICK £1 COIN HERE
(for poster only)

Only need a few Mr. Men or Little Miss to complete your set? You can order any of the titles on the back of the books from our Mr. Men order line on 0870 787 1724. Orders should be delivered between 5 and 7 working days.

TO BE COMPLETED BY AN ADULT

To apply for any of these great offers, ask an adult to complete the details below and send this whole page with the appropriate payment and tokens, to: MR. MEN CLASSIC OFFER, PO BOX 715, HORSHAM RH12 5WG

☐ Please send me a giant-sized double-sided collectors' poster.
AND ☐ I enclose 6 tokens and have taped a £1 coin to the other side of this page.

☐ Please send me ☐ Mr. Men Library case(s) and/or ☐ Little Miss library case(s) at £5.99 each inc P&P

☐ I enclose a cheque/postal order payable to Egmont UK Limited for £............................

OR ☐ Please debit my MasterCard / Visa / Maestro / Delta account (delete as appropriate) for £............................

Card no. ☐☐☐☐ ☐☐☐☐ ☐☐☐☐ ☐☐☐☐ ☐☐☐☐ ☐☐☐☐   Security code ☐☐☐

Issue no. (if available) ☐   Start Date ☐☐/☐☐/☐☐   Expiry Date ☐☐/☐☐/☐☐

Fan's name: ....   Date of birth: ....

Address: ....

....

....   Postcode: ....

Name of parent / guardian: ....

Email for parent / guardian: ....

Signature of parent / guardian: ....

Please allow 28 days for delivery. Offer is only available while stocks last. We reserve the right to change the terms of this offer at any time and we offer a 14 day money back guarantee. This does not affect your statutory rights. Offers apply to UK only.

☐ We may occasionally wish to send you information about other Egmont children's books.
If you would rather we didn't, please tick this box.

Ref: MRM 001

cut along the dotted line and return this whole page